The Magic Potions Shop

The Emerald Dragon

For my Grandma – L.B.

For the Potions Shop Team – you're all magic – A.L.

RED FOX

UK | USA | Canada | Ireland | Australia
India | New Zealand | South Africa

Red Fox is part of the Penguin Random House group of companies
whose addresses can be found at global.penguinrandomhouse.com.

www.penguin.co.uk
www.puffin.co.uk
www.ladybird.co.uk

Penguin
Random House
UK

First published 2017

001

Text copyright © Abie Longstaff, 2017
Illustrations copyright © Lauren Beard and
Penguin Random House Children's UK, 2017

The moral right of the author and illustrator has been asserted

Set in Palatino Regular 16/23pt
Printed in Great Britain by Clays Ltd, St Ives plc

A CIP catalogue record for this book is available from the British Library

ISBN: 978–1–782–95194–0

All correspondence to:
Red Fox
Penguin Random House Children's
80 Strand, London WC2R 0RL

The Magic Potions Shop

The Emerald Dragon

Abie Longstaff & Lauren Beard

RED FOX

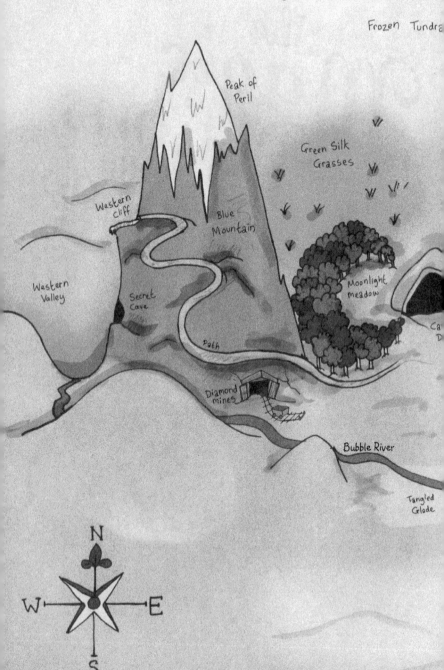

Prince Oro's Palace

Lake Sapphire

The Potions Tree

Steadysong Forest

Troll Hills

Vale of Years

Eastern Shores

Fickle Ocean

Troll Bridge

Troll Plains

Mouse Pond

Vine Curtain

Parched Desert

Chapter One

A dark storm cloud covered the Kingdom of Arthwen, thick and menacing. Down it sank, past the Peak of Peril, covering the Sky Cats and Fluff Griffins. Lower and lower it fell, filling Moonlight Meadow and scaring the Twilight Unicorns into hiding. It dropped until it smothered the grass, and every plant, every living creature, was sucked into its blackness . . .

Tibben sat bolt upright in his little bed at the top of the tree. His heart was thudding. He ran to the window and looked out. There below him the land was still and clear and the sun was rising in the hazy sky. Tibben slumped down in relief. It was just a nightmare!

He breathed in and out to calm himself. Slowly his heart rate returned to normal, but he couldn't shake the funny feeling that something was unsettled – something was off balance.

As Tibben pulled on his cloak, his five Glints sparkled in the morning light. Glints were the magical sign of potions skill; Grandpa's cloak was covered in them! As Potions Master, Grandpa had helped the creatures of Arthwen for many, many years. But last week Grandpa had turned a hundred years old. Soon it would be time for him to retire. Then Tibben, the Potions Apprentice, would take the

Master's Challenge to become a
Potions Master himself.

Tibben knocked on the door to
Grandpa's room. As it swung open,
the first thing he saw was Grandpa,
wearing a plain brown cloak.

Tibben gasped. Grandpa's cloak
had stopped sparkling! All the
Glints had disappeared.

"Your **Glints**!" he cried.

"Yes," said the old
pixie softly. "I'm
no longer the
Potions
Master."

Tibben looked at him in panic. "But wait . . . no!" he cried. "I haven't taken the Master's Challenge. I don't even know what I have to do!"

"Tibben, it's OK," said Grandpa. "Someone will bring the scroll soon, and it will set out the Challenge for you. When it comes, you need to think calmly and clearly. But also quickly . . ."

Tibben's eyes widened.

"Remember, Tibben, in Arthwen there are two energies at work."

He nodded. Grandpa had told him this many times.

"One is Harmony," Grandpa continued, "and the other is Blight."

Tibben shivered. He knew what Blight felt like. Blight was a thick cloud of sadness and emptiness.

Grandpa took his hand. "The gap between Potions Masters is the most dangerous time for Arthwen." He looked at Tibben closely. "Where there is a gap, Blight will fill it." Tibben stared back.

"This Blight will be worse than anything you have ever felt before," his teacher said in a low voice. "It will fall on Arthwen like a dark cloud. You must pass the Challenge as quickly as you can, Tibben."

Tibben trembled as he remembered his nightmare.

"I know you can do it." Grandpa

squeezed his hand. "And I will be waiting for you in the Vale of Years."

A ball of white fluff came bouncing in. It was Wizz. Wizz lived above the Potions Shop with Grandpa and Tibben. She was a Gatherer – someone with a special talent for finding potions ingredients.

Wizz's blue eyes grew wide at the sight of Grandpa's cloak. "Glint gone weez!" she cried.

Grandpa hugged her and smiled. "And it's time for me to go too," he told her. "Goodbye, little Wizz."

There was a rustle outside
Grandpa's window, and an
enormous face appeared, filling
the window frame. It was Cragg,
the Quarry Troll. He was as tall
as the Potions Tree! His huge eyes
twinkled hello.

"Ah, Cragg," said Grandpa. "Thank you for offering to give me a lift."

Cragg smiled and held out his massive finger. Grandpa climbed on and was lifted up to the troll's shoulder.

"Good luck!" he called. "Keep calm, Tibben. Don't panic. Read the recipes carefully. Think of what will help Harmony!"

Grandpa's voice grew fainter as he was carried away through Steadysong Forest towards the Vale of Years.

Chapter Two

The bluebell of the Potions
Shop jangled, and
Tibben's heart jumped.
Could that be someone
bringing the Master's
Challenge? He raced downstairs
and opened the door.

"Good morning, Tibben," said a
low voice. It was Kenta, one of the
centaurs from Moonlight Meadow.
She galloped into the shop, her

sharp hooves clattering on the wooden floor.

"Hello wooz!" said Wizz.

Tibben's heart slowed down – it was just a customer. Of course, the Potions Shop had to carry on as usual.

"How can we help?" he asked.

"My flute doesn't sound right."
Kenta lifted a long silver object
to her lips and blew. A strange-
sounding note came out; she flicked
her tail crossly. "You see?" she said.

"Hmm," said Tibben.

He opened *The Book of
Potions* and turned to:

Sweet Tune Potion

EFFECT: Makes beautiful music

INGREDIENTS:
Light Puff
True Scale
Blue Air

Wizz jumped up right away to fetch the ingredients, bouncing up and down the shelves until she had laid everything out on the wooden counter.

Tibben felt nervous. It was strange making potions without Grandpa in the shop. He pounded the **True Scale** in his **Mage Nut** bowl and added the wisps of *Light Puff*.

He broke open a husk containing Blue Aiv, and it floated over the bowl like a mist.

Tibben tried to stir the potion. "Hmm," he said. He couldn't get the ingredients to blend properly. They were so light and airy! Tibben thought for a moment – just as Grandpa had taught him – and added a drop of water. The Blue Air immediately settled into the bowl and the mixture formed a bright blue liquid.

"That's it!" Tibben smiled. He painted the flute with blue potion. To his surprise it flipped into the air. Then it flopped onto the counter.

"Whaaaat?" Tibben frowned.

He watched in amazement as the flute grew a tail.

"Fish weez?" said Wizz, and Tibben nodded, puzzled. Now the flute really did look like a long fish.

Wizz picked it up and put it in the fish tank above the counter. The flute swam about happily amongst the floating *Cloud Lotus*.

"Um . . . I'm sorry," said Tibben. "I don't know what happened . . ." But he looked round to find Kenta laughing.

"I've never seen a flute swim before!" she chuckled.

Tibben returned to *The Book of Potions*. Underneath the recipe he spotted something. It said:

When combined with liquid,
this potion makes Fishtail Brew,
for swimming and breathing
under water. Lasts for five minutes.

"Oops," said Tibben. "Um . . . let's wait five minutes; then I'll try again."

Kenta giggled as the happy flute-fish did backstroke in the fish tank.

Hee hee!

Chapter Three

Tibben and Wizz were busy for
the rest of the morning. The shop
was full of customers coming in for
potions. Tibben had never seen it
so hectic! There was a restlessness
in the air, and everyone looked
worried.

After lunch the door opened for
what seemed like the hundredth
time. Tibben gasped. There before
him was a very special bird, with

flaming feathers of orange and yellow and red.

"Seraphin?" asked Tibben. "Is that you?" He couldn't believe his eyes – the Firebird was tiny! Last time he saw her she had been enormous!

"It's me," Seraphin said in a soft voice.

Tibben gazed at her in amazement. Seraphin was one of the special creatures of Arthwen. She brought warmth and energy to the kingdom. Every hundred years she built a special nest, filled it with magic fire, and let the flames turn her back into an egg. Then she hatched out as a new

Firebird and started her life all over again.

The little Firebird hopped across the wooden floor of the shop. "Tibben," she said solemnly, "I have brought the Master's Challenge."

Tibben's heart leaped. Seraphin reached under her wing and handed him a scroll of **Silent Bark**. Slowly Tibben unrolled it.

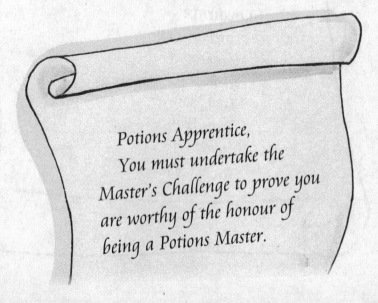

Potions Apprentice,
You must undertake the
Master's Challenge to prove you
are worthy of the honour of
being a Potions Master.

You may ask for help from any creature you wish, except for the former Potions Master.

For the Challenge, you must make a very special potion.

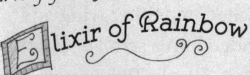

Elixir of Rainbow

Effect: Restores Harmony

Ingredients:

Lavender Cup

Sky Feather

Ice Reed

Troll Moss

Dune Leaf

Sunset Fern

Ruby's Shine

Tibben had never heard of any of the ingredients. "Do you know any of these, Wizz?" he asked.

"No weez, but Wizz find," she said firmly.

"Really?" said Tibben. "Where do they come from?"

Wizz closed her eyes for a moment. Then she ran her finger down the list: "Lake wooz, Peak-a-wooz, Tundra, wooz-a-Bridge, Desert wooz, Tangle-Tangle wooz."

Then Wizz frowned and pointed to the last ingredient.

"*Ruby's Shine*?" asked Tibben. "Do you know that one, Wizz?"

Wizz shook her head. "No weez."

"It sounds like a jewel," said Tibben. "Seraphin, have you heard of *Ruby's Shine*?"

The Firebird shook her head slowly. "I'm afraid not," she said. "But I don't know any of the other ingredients either. They must be very rare."

"Rare wooz." Wizz nodded. "Far, far." She spread her paws wide.

"Yes," said Tibben, "they come from all over the kingdom."

Grandpa had told him he had to be quick. Tibben frowned. "I don't think we'll have time to pick them all."

"I'm sorry I can't fly you," said Seraphin. "I'm still too small."

"No . . ." said Tibben. "You can't" – he thought for a moment – "but maybe someone else could . . ." Seeing the Firebird reminded him of another special creature of Arthwen: Darnöf the Emerald Dragon. Tibben had met him once before.

"Do you think Darnöf would help us?" he said.

"Yes," Seraphin answered quickly. "We four will always work together to keep Harmony."

"Four?" Tibben was confused. He knew the Firebird brought warmth, Darnöf looked after the skies, and the River Horse kept the waters flowing – but that only made three. Who was the fourth special creature of Arthwen?

Tibben looked puzzled, but Wizz jumped up. "Tib Tib," she said firmly.

"Yes." Seraphin nodded. "The Potions Master is the fourth special creature of Arthwen. As Potions Master, you will look after the earth and plants and creatures."

Tibben's eyes widened.

"You are lucky to have a Gatherer to help you," said the Firebird softly, smiling at Wizz.

Tibben was pale. He looked down, wringing his hands. He tried to take it all in – the ingredients, the Challenge, the weight of responsibility on his shoulders.

Wizz took his hand in her paw. "Dragon wooz," she said gently.

"Yes." Tibben slowly came to his senses. "Let's go and see Darnöf."

Chapter Four

Seraphin hung a sign from the
bluebell:

Shop closed
for urgent
business

Tibben and Wizz rushed around
packing ingredients, potions and
warm clothes for their journey.
When their bags were full, they
closed the door and locked it
behind them.

Tibben bowed low to the Firebird, and Seraphin bowed back. "Good luck!" She flapped goodbye with her wing.

Tibben and Wizz headed westwards through Steadysong Forest. Wizz danced here and there,

sniffing at the trees and the ground.

At Lake Sapphire, Wizz cried out and darted over to the edge. She came back with a violet-coloured mushroom in her paw.

"What's that, Wizz?" asked Tibben.

"Cup-cup wooz," she answered, pointing to the scroll where it said Lavender Cup.

Tibben beamed. They had the first ingredient!

They crossed Sapphire Bridge and came to the entrance of the Cave of Darkness.

Tibben coughed nervously.

"Darnöf?" he called. "Are you home?"

There was a rumble from the cave and Tibben saw a large shape moving towards them. It was the dragon! He towered over Tibben, his scales glittering in the low light like thousands of emeralds.

"Ah, young Tibben," he said in his gravelly, growly voice.

Tibben bowed. "Darnöf, it's good to see you again. This is Wizz." He introduced his friend.

Darnöf bowed. "This is an honour," he rumbled. "I have seen four Potions Masters come and go in my lifetime, but I have never met a Gatherer."

Wizz smiled.

"We have a favour to ask you," said Tibben, as Wizz unrolled the scroll to show Darnöf. "We have to

collect these ingredients to make the special potion for the Master's Challenge, but they are spread all over the kingdom."

"Too far weez." Wizz shook her head.

"Please could you fly us?" asked Tibben nervously.

Darnöf nodded. "I will," he said. "But you have to hold on tight. I fly fast."

Tibben looked at Wizz. She was grinning in excitement.

Chapter Five

Tibben sat high on Darnöf's back
and held on as tightly as he could.
Wizz perched in front of him, her
tail wrapped round his wrist.

"Where to?" asked Darnöf.

Tibben thought for a moment,
remembering his dreams. "Grandpa
told us the cloud of Blight would
fall on Arthwen," he said in a
serious voice. "So I think we should
start with the highest part of the

kingdom while we still have time."

"Peak-a-wooz," said Wizz.

"Is that for the **Sky Feather**?" Tibben asked, and she nodded.

The Peak of Peril! Tibben felt a chill run down his spine. He had never been to the peak – it was right at the top of Blue Mountain!

Darnöf spread out his mighty wings and

Whoosh!

He shot up into the air.

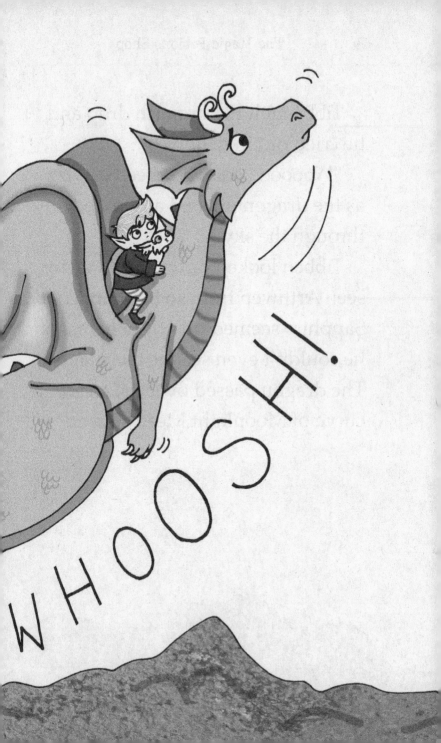

Tibben felt his stomach drop and he cried out in delight.

"Wooooo zooooo!" cheered Wizz as the dragon pitched and rolled through the sky.

Tibben looked down – he'd never seen Arthwen from so high up! Lake Sapphire seemed tiny from here, and he couldn't even see the mermaids. The dragon passed over the crescent curve of Moonlight Meadow, and

then over the Green Silk Grasses.
In no time at all they had reached
the Peak of Peril.

All of a sudden a panicked look
came across Wizz's face. "Weez!"
she cried, and Tibben followed her
paw as she pointed up. In the sky a
dark cloud floated over Arthwen.

"Blight," he breathed. He had felt
Blight before. He had seen its effects
on the kingdom. But he had never

seen Blight look like this! It was as bad as in his nightmare – a dense, dark cloud radiating sadness.

"Yes," said Darnöf. "It has been falling closer all week."

"Wh-what do we do?" Tibben's voice shook.

"We fight it," the dragon said simply. He took a deep breath and blew a long stream of fire up into the sky. The dark cloud was pushed back by the warmth and light.

"Wow!" cried Tibben.

"That will hold it back a little," said

Darnöf. "But not for long. Arthwen needs a Potions Master."

"I am going to pass the Challenge," Tibben said grimly, and he gripped Wizz tighter as Darnöf swooped down to land in the snow at the top of Blue Mountain.

Immediately, Wizz bounced off, sniffing and darting about, trying to find the **Sky Feather.** Tibben turned round slowly. "Something feels wrong," he said.

Just then there was a rumble and the peak began to shake! Tibben and Wizz were thrown to the ground as the snow slid out from under them.

Tibben grabbed a large rock and Wizz clung to his arm with her tail. Darnöf flew up into the air to escape.

Then, as quickly as it had begun, the shaking stopped.

"What happened?" said Tibben.

"Blight is affecting everything in the land," Darnöf explained. "There is no ground you can be sure of."

Tibben heard a muffled cry from under the snow. Something was stuck beneath the avalanche!

"Here wooz," said Wizz, pointing down with her paw.

"Darnöf!" cried Tibben. "We need some of your fire!"

The dragon blew softly onto the snow. It melted away to reveal a bright blue Fluff Griffin. He was sitting on a nest of eggs, looking stunned.

Gently Tibben lifted him out.

The bird shook his head as if to clear it and bowed to Tibben and Darnöf in thanks. He offered Tibben a bright blue feather.

The moment Wizz saw it she squealed and jumped up and down.

"Is this a **Sky Feather**?" Tibben asked, and Wizz nodded in excitement.

"We've got the second ingredient!" he cried. He turned to the Fluff Griffin and bowed. "Thank you," he said, a huge smile on his face.

"Where next?" asked Darnöf.

"Tundra," said Wizz, holding the list, and the two friends climbed onto the dragon's back. They held on tight as Darnöf turned north.

Tibben glanced up – the storm cloud was lower now, it had dropped to cover the Peak of Peril. Over his shoulder, Tibben could see the peak shaking again.

"We have to hurry," he said.

"Did someone say hurry?" said Darnöf. "Here we go!"

Chapter Six

Tibben could barely breathe as
the dragon leaned into the air and
burst through the sky. He'd never
imagined travelling so fast! His
cheeks were stretched taut and his
mouth split open in a wide grin.

In no time at all they had flown the
length of Arthwen, gathering Ice Reed
in the Frozen Tundra, Troll Moss
from underneath Troll Bridge, and
Dune Leaf from the Parched Desert.

Everywhere they went they were called upon by the creatures of Arthwen for help. Everywhere they went Tibben saw signs of Blight. The tundra was melting into slush, the mighty Troll Bridge was crumbling away and the desert was dry as dust. Tears filled Tibben's eyes. His beloved Arthwen was falling apart!

Wizz touched his hand with her soft paw. "Nearly there-there."

Tibben nodded. There were only two more ingredients left to find: Sunset Fern in the Tangled Glade, and the mysterious

Ruby's Shine. In each place they visited Tibben had asked about *Ruby's Shine*, but no one knew what it was. Nor had Wizz sensed it.

All the while, Blight was growing. The dark cloud was sinking down and down. By the time they reached the Tangled Glade, it was so low that Darnöf hardly had space to fly. He staggered the last few metres, bumping along the ground to come to a halt.

"I can't fly you any further," he said. He lifted his emerald head and blew, but the Blight was so strong now his fiery breath wasn't able to push back the fog. He lay down to rest.

"Thank you, Darnöf." Tibben tried to smile. "You've done all you can." His heart was pounding. How would they manage without the dragon?

The cloud overhead was almost blocking the sun and the land was growing dark. Tibben could hardly see through the fog of Blight.

"Are you all right, Wizz?" he called through the dusky air.

"Wizz good!" came an excited squeal from behind him, and through the gloom Tibben could just make out the shape of Wizz, holding something bright orange.

"Fern wooz!" she cried.

Tibben's face broke into a grin.

Sunset Fern! The sixth ingredient.
Now they just needed Ruby's
Shine.

"Can you sense Ruby's Shine
here, Wizz?" he asked.

She shook her head.

Tibben looked down. In the dim
light he could see his five **Glints**
sparkling up at him. He touched the
fourth **Glint** – Ruby level – and ran
his finger over its shiny red surface.
He still felt sure Ruby's Shine was
a jewel. It had to be. Who would
know about jewels? Who could
he ask?

There were Thunder Goblins in
the diamond mines at the base of
Blue Mountain, but Tibben shook

his head; they only knew about
diamonds, not rubies.

Tibben rubbed his chin . . . "Oh!"
An idea suddenly came to him.
"Prince Oro!"

If anyone knew about jewels, it
would be the Golden Prince! He
loved anything shiny, especially gold
and jewels. Oro might even own
Ruby's Shine himself!

"Let's go to the palace!" said
Tibben. He pulled out his map
and peered at it through the fog.
His heart sank. It was miles away.
Without Darnöf they'd have to walk
– and walk fast.

"Hmm," he mused. "I wonder . . ."
He traced his finger from the

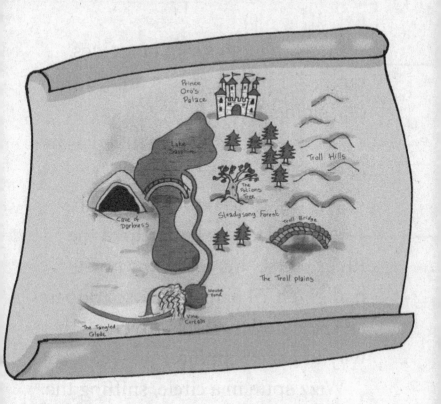

Tangled Glade, along Bubble River and through Lake Sapphire to the north-east point. "The water goes all the way to the palace," he said.

Wizz looked at him. "Swim weez?" She looked puzzled.

"It's too far to swim ourselves, but . . ." Tibben's eyes searched the darkening glade.

"Horse weez?" Wizz smiled as he nodded.

The last time Tibben was in the Tangled Glade he had helped the River Horse. In return, the horse had given Tibben and Wizz a super-fast ride down Bubble River, all the way to Lake Sapphire!

Wizz spun in a circle, sniffing the air to find the horse.

"Not here wooz." She shook her head.

"May I?" Darnöf stepped forward. He gave a powerful

Roar!

From downriver came an answering whinny.

Moments later there was a splash, and out of the mist came a tall creature. His coat shone creamy silver and his mane shimmered in the fading light. It was the River Horse!

"It is good to see you," the pixie said. He bowed to the mighty horse, and the horse bowed back. "Please could you help us?" Tibben asked. "We're trying to get to Prince Oro's palace."

The horse nodded his silver head and motioned towards his back.

Tibben grinned. The River Horse was offering them a ride!

"Thank you," he said with a smile. Tibben swung himself onto the horse's back and Wizz clambered up in front of him.

"Goodbye, Darnöf," said Tibben
as they rode away. "Thank you for
your help."

"Good luck, little pixie," the
dragon called out through the fog.

Chapter Seven

Whoosh!

They were off! Speeding down
Bubble River, the hooves of the River
Horse stomped and splashed though
the water.

In no time at all, Tibben found
himself at the north-east edge of Lake
Sapphire, just outside the palace.

He and Wizz ran through the
golden gates and up the path as fast
as they could.

The fancy door opened, and a pool of light spilled out. Prince Oro stood there, smiling.

"Hey," he said.

Tibben's eyes widened. The Golden Prince looked completely different! Gone were the jewels and elegant clothes. He stood before them in ordinary clothes; the only shiny thing was a crown on his head. Tibben grinned – the prince looked great!

"I was just baking some cupcakes," Oro

drawled. "Do you want one?"

"Sorry, Oro, we don't have long," said Tibben. "We're looking for something to complete the Master's Challenge. Have you heard of *Ruby's Shine?*"

Oro shook his head straight away.

Tibben's heart sank. Time was running out! "We think it might be a jewel," he tried again.

"A jewel?" Oro screwed up his face in thought.

"We've tried everywhere," said Tibben. "The forest, the mountains, the snow, the desert, the glade, the river."

"Not ocean-wooz," said Wizz suddenly.

"What's that, Wizz?" Tibben stared at her. Slowly he realized she was right: the Fickle Ocean was the only place they hadn't tried. "The Fickle Ocean," he breathed.

"Oh! I know, I know!" Prince Oro shot off down the palace corridor.

A few moments later he came dashing back, a big book in his hands.

On the cover it said:

The Hunt for Red Octavia

"The *Red Octavia* was an enormous treasure ship," the prince said, all in a rush. "It was carrying the largest cargo of rubies the kingdom has ever seen . . ."

He flicked through the pages of the book as he spoke. "But it hit a storm and sank to the bottom of the Fickle Ocean. And no one has seen it since!" He opened the book wide to show Tibben.

There before him was a picture of a beautiful old ship. On its deck were wooden chests with open lids. Tibben leaned in closer . . .

"Rubies!" he breathed. The chests were full of thousands of rubies!

Tibben looked at the Gatherer. "What do you think, Wizz?"

She closed her eyes, then held up a paw to the book. "Yes wooz," she said. "*Ruby* maybe there."

"Do you think your Gathering will work underwater?" asked Tibben.

"Yes," said Wizz firmly. "Come, come." She took his hand.

"Thank you, Oro!" Tibben called over his shoulder as he was yanked along the corridor.

"Weez!" Wizz cried out as she opened the palace door. The cloud of Blight had come right down! The air before them was now dark and thick.

Tibben began to panic. He felt like he'd been sucked into a well of blackness. His mind felt fuzzy, making it hard to think clearly. His heart sank. It was hopeless. They'd never find *Ruby's Shine*. He'd never be a Potions Master.

"No!" He shook his head firmly.

Blight would not win.

"I am going to pass the Challenge!" he called out into the fog. To his amazement, his words pushed the cloud back a little - just as Darnöf's breath had done. Tibben felt his heart lift – he had an idea. He rummaged in his bag for a bottle of yellow liquid.

"Yes!" he cried. "I thought I had some Lightcast Potion!" He took a sip. Suddenly a circle of bright light appeared on the ground around them.

Tibben set his jaw and held Wizz's paw tight. "Come on, Wizz, we can do this," he said firmly.

"Yes wooz!" shouted Wizz, and

the cloud was pushed further back.

Tibben's heart swelled with hope.

Together the friends ran, hand in paw, all the way to Lake Sapphire.

The River Horse was waiting next to the water.

"Please . . ." Tibben gasped, out of breath. "We need to go to the Fickle Ocean."

But the horse only frowned.

Tibben turned, and saw that the Blight had closed in. They were completely surrounded by inky blackness. The only light came from the small circle around them.

A tear ran down the cheek of the mighty horse.

"Don't give up." Tibben looked into the horse's eyes. "There must be a way through," he said gently. "My potion will light us."

The River Horse gave a low whinny. He tossed his silver mane and stamped his foot.

"Have you got an idea?" Tibben asked, and the great horse nodded.

Tibben grinned at Wizz.

In a flash they had climbed onto the horse's back and . . . they were off!

Chapter Eight

Tibben had thought that, by now, he knew every inch of Arthwen. He thought he had been to every mountain, every valley and every river. But as the River Horse swam to the northernmost corner of Lake Sapphire, Tibben realized he was wrong. Here, there were high cliffs that towered over the edge of the lake. Through the darkness he spotted something he'd never seen before. The lake water was running right into a cave at the base of the cliffs. Arthwen had an underground river!

"Does this river go all the way to the Fickle Ocean?" Tibben asked, and the horse nodded.

"Wooooz!" cried Wizz in amazement and Tibben grinned. An underground river! They could escape the Blight!

He hung on tight as the horse swam swiftly into the dark tunnel. Away from the Blight, Tibben's mind cleared. He breathed in deeply and hugged his friend.

The sound of splashing echoed off the walls as they passed under

Arthwen, following the twists and turns of the hidden river. For a while all felt calm, then . . .

Splash!

The horse shot out of the underground river – straight into the Fickle Ocean.

Out on the ocean the air was filled with a dense fog of sorrow. High winds blew and waves pounded into the horse. He fought against the swell.

Tibben felt the despair begin to build again. He choked back tears of frustration and tried to focus. He breathed in and out slowly, filling his mind with peaceful thoughts and pushing the feeling of sadness away. Wizz could find *Ruby's Shine*, he told himself. Wizz could find anything.

His mind clearer, he turned to the Gatherer. "Where to?" he shouted over the wind.

Wizz closed her eyes. She pointed

out to sea, and the River Horse swam through the dark waters, bouncing up and down with the waves.

He swam until Wizz called out: "Stop weez!"

"Here?" said Tibben. They were in the middle of nowhere.

"*Ruby* wooz," said Wizz firmly.

"OK." Tibben nodded. "Let's swim down and see if we can find the *Red Octavia*." He leaned over the side of the horse.

"How deep do you think it is, Wizz?" he asked nervously.

"Long way, wooz," said Wizz.

Tibben frowned. He wasn't sure how long he could hold his breath.

The River Horse couldn't help them – he couldn't breathe underwater either. Tibben shook his head. There had to be something he could do . . .

Then his face cleared – he remembered! That very morning he had made Fishtail Brew by accident! He smiled as he thought of the flute-fish swimming around, and fumbled in his bag for the potion.

"This will let us breathe underwater," he said, holding out the bottle for Wizz to sip. "We have to hurry," he warned. "The potion only works for five minutes."

She squeezed Tibben's hand and slipped off the horse into the cold water. All at once she gave a little

cry and flipped over.
Tibben laughed –
Wizz had grown
a scaly fish tail!

Now he took
a quick sip
of *Lightcast
Potion* and then
swallowed the rest of the *Fishtail Brew*.

Instantly he felt
his legs stick
fast together. He
looked down and,
instead of feet,
saw a floppy tail!

Tibben felt his neck – there were little bumps on the side – he had gills! All of a sudden he found breathing air difficult.

Tibben waved goodbye to the River Horse and followed Wizz into the cold murky ocean. Nervously, he tried a breath. His potion worked! He could breathe underwater! He gave Wizz a thumbs-up. She smiled back at him.

Deeper and deeper they swam, searching for the ship.

Tibben saw that Wizz's eyes were closed as she sensed where she needed to go, and her whiskers were twitching under the water. She yanked him to the side, the circle of

The Emerald Dragon

Lightcast Potion surrounding them as they swam down.

Soon Tibben saw where Wizz was heading. He gasped in amazement. There, perched on an underwater cliff, was an old wooden ship! It was covered in a red plant that twisted and turned, snaking in and out of cracks in the ancient planks. Tiny orange fish peeped out at them, hiding behind the scarlet leaves.

Tibben pushed the plant out of the way and, painted on the wood, saw the words:

Red Octavia

Wizz had found the treasure ship!
Surely *Ruby's Shine* would be on
it!

They swam to the deck. Wizz's
tail pricked up, and all in a rush she
moved over to a large chest. It was
covered in more of the red plant,
its strands wrapped round the lid.
Tibben pulled the plant away and
Wizz yanked open the lid. They
leaned over to see what was inside.

The chest was full of rubies!

"*Ruby's Shine!*" Tibben's voice
came out strangely underwater – like
it was full of bubbles. He beamed at
Wizz and she smiled back. The pixie
loaded his arms with as many jewels
as he could carry.

He could feel the Fishtail Brew
beginning to wear off. His tail began
to separate out into two legs again.
His gills tightened. "Hurry!" he cried.
Tibben took a deep breath to make sure
he had enough air to get himself all the
way back to the surface.

Just as they were about to swim up,
a giant Brine Serpent floated by. It came
towards the Lightcast circle, its tail
flicking back and forth in the water as
it swam: flick, flick, flick, **CRASH!**

The heavy tail hit the mast of the
Red Octavia, knocking the ship and
throwing Tibben aside. He clutched the
jewels tightly, but lost sight of Wizz.

The enormous mast began to creak
and groan.

"Wizz!" Tibben shouted a bubble of noise. There she was! Right by the mighty mast! He watched in horror as it fell, heading straight towards her.

"Wizz!" he burbled in panic. Without a second thought he dropped the jewels and swam straight for his friend. Grabbing her paw, he pulled her out of the way just in time as the mast crashed through the deck causing the ship to topple and slowly slide off the edge of cliff. Tibben's fish tail was almost gone and his lungs were burning for air. He could feel the currents around the ship trying to suck them further down. He watched in despair as the pile of jewels sank to the bottom of the ocean.

Tibben turned away from the *Ruby's Shine*. He pulled, Wizz kicked, and together – with their last ounce of strength – they swam up to the surface and let the waves carry them ashore.

Chapter Nine

Tibben and Wizz lay on the wet
sand of the Eastern Shores, looking
up at the inky cloud. There was a
loud roll of thunder, and a streak
of lightning cut across the black
fog in a sharp, jagged spike. Tears
fell down Tibben's cheeks. He had
failed the Master's Challenge. Now
there was no Potions Master, and
Blight had filled Arthwen.

The little pixie looked at his

friend. Even though he felt a deep swell of shame inside, he didn't regret saving Wizz. He couldn't have left her there under the ocean. She was his best friend, his team-mate. Even through his tears Tibben knew he would choose Wizz over the jewels every single time.

Tibben heard a great thundering of hooves and feet. He sat up. Word had spread that the Potions Apprentice was down at the Fickle Ocean, and creatures were coming from far and wide to watch him complete the Master's Challenge. Tibben shook his head; little did they know that he had already failed!

Through the storm he could see

hundreds of flaming torches held by Quarry Trolls and Sand Elves and mermaids and Shadow Owls and Thunder Goblins and Dancing Stags and Silver Squirrels. There was King Krono and Prince Oro and Karhu, the Blizzard Bear, all waiting for him to become the Potions Master. He hung his head. He had let everyone down.

Wizz's fur was still wet from the ocean, and bits of the red plant were entangled in the tufts on her head.

She pushed the plant aside.

As she touched it, her eyes widened. Wizz jumped up in the air, her tail raised and her whiskers taut.

"*Shine* wooz!" she cried, her eyes sparkling.

"What?" said Tibben, puzzled.

"*Shine* wooz!" Wizz bounced around, squealing. "*Shine* wooz! *Shine* wooz!" She said it over and over.

Slowly it dawned on Tibben what she was saying. He could hardly believe it.

"Wizz." He stopped her with his hands on her shoulders. "Are you saying this red plant is *Ruby's Shine*?"

Wizz nodded, beaming.

"Yes!" Tibben cried. *Ruby's Shine* wasn't a jewel! It was a plant! The red plant that had covered the ship. They had all the ingredients! They could make the potion.

His hands shaking, Tibben untied his **Mage Nut** bowl from his bag.

The creatures of Arthwen gathered round, holding their torches high. Something special was going to happen.

Tibben pulled the seven ingredients out of his backpack. Then he took another sip of *Lightcast Potion.* "I'm ready to

make the *Elixir of Rainbow,"*
he said solemnly.

He thought of all the training that
had led up to this point. He thought
of Grandpa, of the lessons the wise
old pixie had taught him. He was
ready.

Then he read the recipe through
again. This time he read to the very
end and, at the bottom, spotted a
note he had not seen before. It said:

*All the ingredients
must be added in order.*

Tibben's heart stopped. In order?
What did that mean? What order?
He could feel himself beginning to
panic. But he closed his eyes and

breathed in and out slowly. Then he looked down at the ingredients, from the blue **Sky Feather** to the red *Ruby's Shine*, and suddenly he realized.

The red
Ruby's Shine

The orange
Sunset Fern

The yellow
Dune Leaf

"Wizz! We have all the colours of the rainbow."

Together, the Potions Apprentice and the Gatherer lined up the ingredients:

The green
Troll Moss

The blue
Sky Feather

The indigo
Ice Reed

The violet
Lavender Cup

One by one Tibben put them into his **Mage Nut** bowl, mushing and pounding and chopping and peeling. As he stirred, the pixie closed his eyes and thought of Harmony. He thought about the land and the plants and all the special creatures joined together.

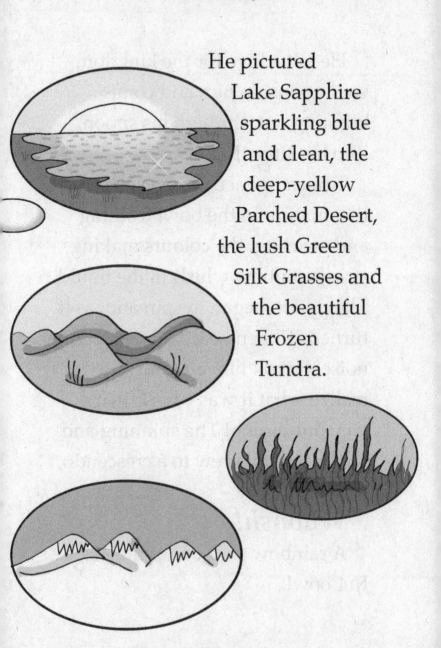

He pictured Lake Sapphire sparkling blue and clean, the deep-yellow Parched Desert, the lush Green Silk Grasses and the beautiful Frozen Tundra.

He felt a love for the kingdom well up inside him and come bursting out, through his spoon, into his **Mage Nut** bowl.

Tibben opened his eyes to see the mixture in the bowl frothing and swirling, the colours making stripy rainbow whirls in the liquid. The potion began to spin and, as it turned, Tibben heard a low buzzing noise. It took him a moment to realize what it was – his **Glints** were humming! The spinning and the humming grew to a crescendo, until suddenly –

Whoosh!

A rainbow shot out of the **Mage Nut** bowl.

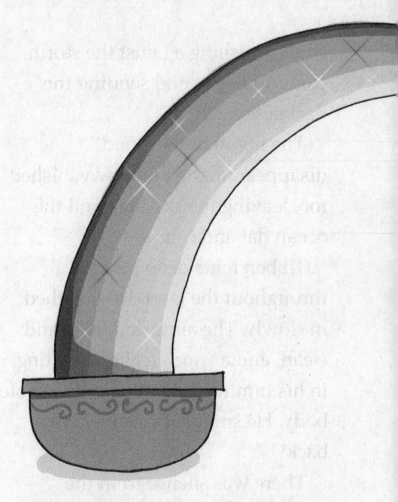

He heard a gasp from the crowd
as everyone gazed at the beautiful
arc. The rays of colour sparkled and

shone, pushing against the storm cloud of Blight and sending the darkness away.

The moment the cloud disappeared, the rainbow vanished too, leaving the sky blue and the ocean flat and calm.

Tibben felt a deep peace throughout the land. He breathed in slowly. The air tasted fresh and clean, and a warm feeling, starting in his tummy, spread over his whole body. He smiled: Harmony was back!

There was silence from the crowd, and then an overwhelming wall of happy noise hit Tibben. The creatures roared, stamped, squeaked and called out in delight. Silver Squirrels waltzed with Twilight Unicorns,

Quarry Trolls lifted Thunder Goblins into the air, Sky Cats and Whistle Birds burst into song.

Everyone cheered and clapped and saluted and bowed to Tibben, and the pixie grinned from ear to ear.

Wizz flung her arms round his neck, nearly knocking him over. He buried his head in her soft fur.

"We did it!" he whispered. "We did it!"

Tibben lifted his head and

scanned the crowd. To one side he saw Oro, waving. Then, next to him, the special creatures of Arthwen: Seraphin the Firebird, Darnöf the Emerald Dragon and the River Horse. They nodded at him and bowed low. Tibben's heart soared.

He looked down. There on his cloak was a new Glint, sparkling with every colour of the rainbow.

Though he was filled with happiness, suddenly there was one person he was desperate to see.

"Darnöf?" He walked over to the dragon. "Please could you take us to the Vale of Years?"

Chapter Ten

Darnöf flew north, from the Eastern Shores to the Vale of Years. From high in the air Tibben could see Arthwen sparkling happily below. He squeezed Wizz tight and smiled into her soft fur.

The dragon swooped down and Tibben saw the lush green grasses below him. It was quiet and peaceful here, the perfect place for Grandpa.

Darnöf landed just outside a little cottage.

"Thank you," said Tibben, bowing to the dragon. "We couldn't have done it without you."

"It was an honour," answered the dragon in his growly voice, and off he flew into the clear Arthwen skies.

Tibben turned to the cottage. Grandpa was waiting in the doorway.

The old pixie beamed, his arms wide open, and Tibben fell into an enormous hug. Grandpa squeezed him tight and Tibben pulled Wizz into the embrace.

"I'm so proud of you both." Grandpa's voice was husky with

tears. "So proud," he said again.

Then he pulled back and took something out of his pocket. It was the *Master's Dial*. It measured Harmony and Blight. "This is yours now," he told Tibben.

"No, no," said Tibben. "The *Dial* belongs to the Potions Master."

Grandpa looked at him closely and Tibben suddenly realized . . .

"That's me!" He looked at Wizz. "Me! I'm the Potions Master!"

Grandpa nodded. "You are," he said, smiling. "And I always knew you would be a great one."

Later, Tibben and Wizz walked all the way back to the Potions

Shop, hand in paw.

Tibben unlocked the door, and together he and Wizz made a brand-new sign. It said:

Tibben and Wizz's Potions Shop

Tibben hung it on the door with pride. He leaned against the doorway, holding Wizz in his arms. The friends watched the setting sun throw its oranges and yellows across the green trees of Steadysong Forest. Everything was peaceful. Everything was in Harmony.

And, even though it was just him and Wizz now, to Tibben it felt like Grandpa would always be there beside them.

Tibben smiled and closed the door of the Potions Shop.

Potions

Elixir of Rainbow

Effect: Restores harmony
Ingredients:

- Lavender Cup
- Sky Feather
- Ice Reed
- Troll Moss
- Dune Leaf
- Sunset Fern
- Ruby's Shine

Sweet Tune Potion

Effect: Makes beautiful music
Ingredients:

- Light Puff
- True Scale
- Blue Air

When combined with liquid, this potion makes Fishtail Brew, for swimming and breathing under water. Lasts for five minutes.

Lightcast Potion

Effect: Creates a circle of light for five minutes
Ingredients:

- Bright Toadstool
- Bat's Tooth

Ingredients

Extracts from
The Glossary of Magic Ingredients

Lavender Cup
Purple-coloured mushroom found at the edge of Lake Sapphire.

Sky Feather
Blue feather. Exchange with **Fluff Griffins** on the Peak of Peril.

Ice Reed
Indigo-coloured plant. Grows in the Frozen Tundra.

Troll Moss
Green moss found under Troll Bridge.

Dune Leaf
Yellow leaf. Grows in the Parched Desert.

Sunset Fern
Orange plant. Grows in the Tangled Glade.

Ruby's Shine
Very rare ingredient. Secret location.

Blue Air
Pick in husks from pine trees on Blue Mountain.

Light Puff
Comes from the breath of a dragon. Used in all Flying Potions, Hover Potions, **Rooting Potion** and **Sweet Tune Potion**.

True Scale
Exchange with Song Fish in the Fickle Ocean. Used in **Sweet Tune Potion** and **Fishtail Potion**.

Bright Toadstool
Grows in Moonlight Meadow, among the pixies. Used in Light Potions and **Dress-Up Potion**.

Bat's Tooth
Exchange with the bats of Troll Hills for **Super Hearing Gel**. Used in Light potions, Seeing potions and **Fortune Teller Cream**.

Grandpa's Quiz

Test your knowledge – how many
questions can you answer?

1. Do you remember how Tibben made
   Fishtail Brew?

First, Tibben pounded the T_____ S_____
in his M_____ N____ bowl.
Next, he added the wisps of L_____ P_____ .
After that, he broke open a husk containing
B_____ A _____ .
Finally, he added a drop of w_____ .

2. Which special creature brings Tibben the
   Master's Challenge?

3. Which special creature flies Tibben
   and Wizz to the Peak of Peril?

4. Which special creature takes Tibben and
   Wizz to the Fickle Ocean?

5. Who is the fourth special creature of the
   Kingdom of Arthwen?

Turn to the back of the book
for the answers to this quiz!

Elixir of Rainbow

Do you recognize the ingredients
of Elixir of Rainbow?

_____ _____ _____

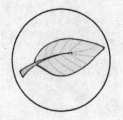

_____ _____

_____ _____

Turn to the back of the book for the answers!

Where in Arthwen?

Where in the Kingdom of Arthwen can you
find the ingredients for Elixir of Rainbow?

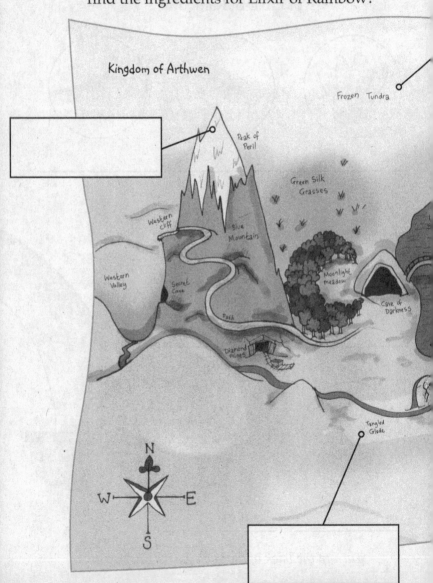

Kingdom of Arthwen

Frozen Tundra

Peak of Peril

Green Silk Grasses

Western Cliff

Blue Mountain

Western Valley

Secret Cave

Moonlight Meadow

Cave of Darkness

Path

Diamond Mines

Tangled Glade

N
W   E
S

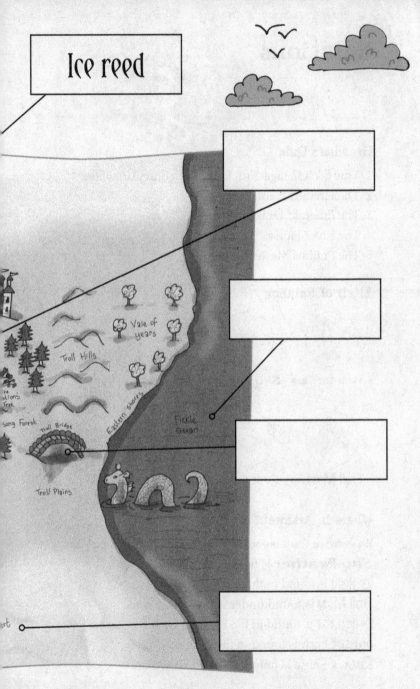

Ice reed

Vale of years

Troll Hills

Troll Bridge

Eastern shores

Fickle Ocean

Troll Plains

Song Forest

Turn to the back of the book for the answers!

Solutions

Grandpa's Quiz

1. True Scale; Mage Nut; Light Puff; Blue Air; water
2. The Firebird (Seraphin)
3. The Emerald Dragon (Darnöf)
4. The River Horse
5. The Potions Master (Tibben)

Elixir of Rainbow

Lavender Cup

Sky Feather

Ice Reed

Troll Moss

Dune Leaf

Sunset Fern

Ruby's Shine

Where in Arthwen?

Lavender Cup is found at the edge of Lake Sapphire.

Sky Feather is found on the Peak of Peril.

Ice Reed is found in the Frozen Tundra.

Troll Moss is found underneath Troll Bridge.

Dune Leaf is found in the Parched Desert.

Sunset Fern is found in the Tangled Glade.

Ruby's Shine is found in the Fickle Ocean.